2013 Xmas,

To Nicholas & Molly

For being good.

MERRY CHRISTMAS!

From Santa
& Nonny & Poppy

Santa's sleigh flew through the starry night, heading south across the Arctic Ocean. On they flew in the crisp, wintry air, crossing over Canada. In the wink of an eye, the sleigh was flying above the Rocky Mountains, and on to New Mexico. The youngest reindeer was very excited. He had never been away from the North Pole before.

From Clovis to Carlsbad, from Ruidoso to Rio Rancho, from Albuquerque to Alamogordo, and ALL the places in between, Santa and his sleigh visited every house in New Mexico.